I TIC

Written by: Abby Hargrove

Illustrated by: Rhema Coleman

Copyright © 2017 by Abby Hargrove
ISBN-13: 978-1974266128
Published by CLC Publishing

I want to dedicate this book to my dad, Jerry Hargrove; my mom, Stacey Hargrove; and my siblings Nicole, Nathan and Matthew, who have learned to roll with each new tic that comes their way and who still love and support me in everything I do.

For more information about Tourette's Syndrome, contact the Tourette's Association of America.

To contact the author, Abby Hargrove, visit: www.facebook.com/iticabby

I Tic

Sometimes I tic.

I bet you are wondering what a tic is. What is a tic?

A tic is a movement that I do with my body, or a sound with my voice, over and over and over again.

**My tic is caused by a
complication in my brain.**

The doctors say the ~~(problem)~~ is
it's called Tourette's Syndrome.

That is a scary sounding word, but it's just a fancy name for a tic.

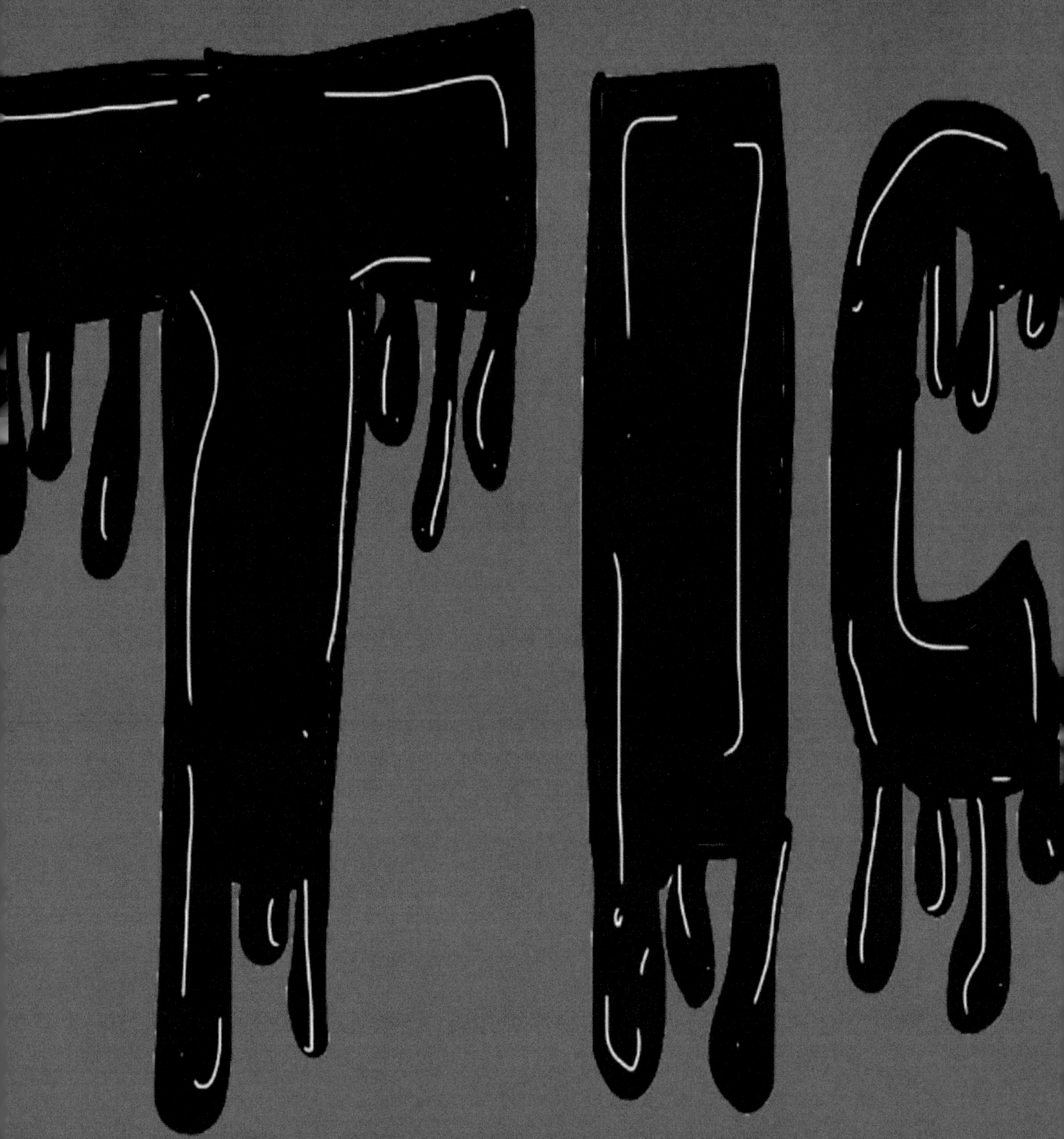

Sometimes people stare at me and on those days, I feel sad.

The worst thing is when a snort, a sniff or a grunt comes pouring out of my mouth and I can't stop it.

Everyone stops and stares at me.

It's hardest when I am at the library and the little old ladies tell me to "Shhhh...Shhhh...Shhhh!!!"

You see, a tic is like a sneeze that I can't hold in, or a hiccup that never goes away.

When one tic starts to go away,
another one just comes along to
take its place.

They never stop. They make me so tired I just want to scream!

I try to hold them in but I can't.

Sometimes I worry other kids will make fun of me. But my friends love me for who I am and never make fun of me!

My friends call me weird, and sometimes they repeat the sounds I make and laugh at me.

But I am special in my very own way.

Instead of crawling under a rug (which is really what I want to do) I hold my head up high, adjust my crown a little straighter.

I know I can do anything I want to do and be anything I want to be!

Someday, I hope to be a horse riding teacher.

I am who I am and I do what I do
because I am me.

I am special and that makes me happy!

Made in the USA
San Bernardino, CA
26 December 2019

62345477R00031